# CONSTRUCTION ZOO

JENNIFER THORNE

PICTURES by
SUSIE HAMMER

Albert Whitman & Company
Chicago, Illinois

Up at the zoo, a quiet morning,
when suddenly, without any warning...

# What's this? Spinning, roaring, crashing–

digging, rolling, growling, smashing!

Animals everywhere wake and skitter
to see what's set the zoo a-flitter.

Big trucks roll 'round hills and bends.
But are they scary—or are they friends?

# Giraffe just craned his neck to see...

a yellow truck, tall as can be.
Its head lifts uuuuuuup into the sky–
the perfect height for giraffe to say, "Hi!"

**Rhino wants to start a fight,**
**then spots a truck–and what a sight.**

Look at its head, so sharp and tough.
This bulldozer's made of sturdy stuff.

The monkeys pace, all worried, antsy,

**but with one swoop, they're happy-dancy!**

Boom! Crash!
Everything falls!

**They're pretty fun, these wrecking balls.**

**Curious elephant can't believe
what this machine has up its sleeve.**

Its trunk can scoop into the ground—
it toots a mighty trumpet sound!

**Giant tortoise wanders close
to scout a truck more loaded than most.**

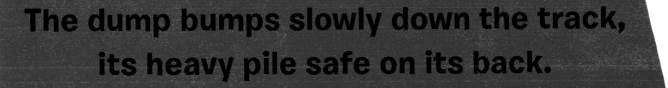

The dump bumps slowly down the track,
its heavy pile safe on its back.

Two tiger brothers crouch and spy
a cement mixer truck set up nearby.

Its striped back spins and rolls all day,
just like the cubs' backs when they play.

Tumbling down hills, digging with snouts,

**running and stretching and making wild shouts.**

Trucks and animals, two by two...

# It's party time at Construction Zoo!

Then one afternoon, the site gets slow.
The trucks pack up—and roll—and go.
It's quiet now up at the zoo.

# The animals aren't sure what to do.

**But here comes zookeeper–
one bright ribbon, a pair of scissors,
and a crowd of guests with him.**

# A snip, a cheer, construction is done.

And now the zoo
is twice the fun!

ZOO

**For Ollie the giraffe–JT**

**To my little sister and big friend Zosia–SH**

Library of Congress Cataloging-in-Publication data is on file with the publisher.

Text copyright © 2018 by Jennifer Thorne
Pictures copyright © 2018 by Susie Hammer
First published in the United States of America in 2018 by Albert Whitman & Company
ISBN 978-0-8075-1282-1

Printed in China
10 9 8 7 6 5 4 3 2 1 WKT 22 21 20 19 18

Design by Morgan Beck

For more information about Albert Whitman & Company,
visit our website at www.albertwhitman.com.